# Party Time, Poppy!

# Party Time, Poppy!

### LUCY DANIELS

#### Illustrated by DAVID MELLING

AN
**APPLE**
PAPERBACK

Scholastic Inc.
New York   Toronto   London   Sydney
Mexico City   New Delhi   Hong Kong   Buenos Aires

To Alexandra Poppy Westrop

Special thanks for Jan Burchett and Sara Vogler

ISBN 0-439-68197-9

Text copyright © 2004 by Working Partners Limited
Created by Working Partners Limited, London W6OQT
Illustrations copyright © 2004 by David Melling

12 11 10 9 8 7 6 5 4 3                    7 8 9 10/0

Printed in the U.S.A.
First Scholastic printing, January 2005

PEBBLE
BEACH

HATTIE

FERGAL

UR
BA

POPPY

REEF

ROCKS
SHIPWRECK

VINNIE

OSCAR

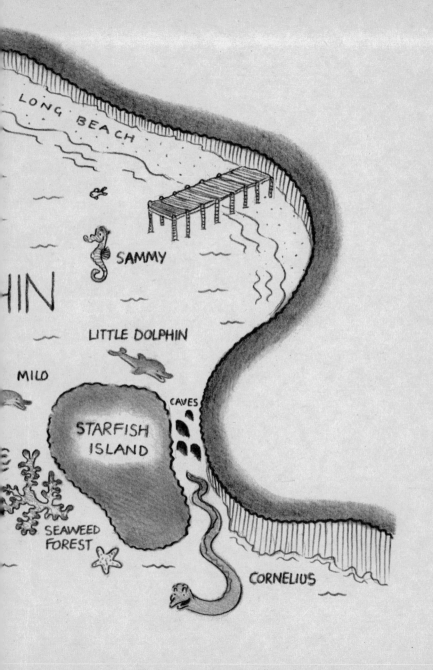

# CHAPTER ONE

Little Dolphin was looking for
Poppy the spinner dolphin. His
best friend, Milo, was helping.
First, Little Dolphin checked behind
the rocks. Then he looked through
the pink fingers of coral growing
out of the reef. "Poppy's not here,
Milo!" he whistled.

There was a gush of bubbles
and Milo burst out from a kelp bush.

1

He shook the floppy leaves off his flippers. "She's not in there, either," he chirped. "I've searched it from top to bottom."

"Good," Little Dolphin said. "If she's nowhere nearby, we can make our plans in secret!"

It was Poppy's birthday tomorrow. Little Dolphin and Milo had decided to have a surprise party for her. All her friends knew they had to keep it a secret from Poppy. But Poppy was the nosiest creature in Urchin Bay! It was hard to keep secrets from her.

Milo was full of great ideas for the party. "We could ask the

seagulls to fly over and make
the word 'Poppy' in the air," he
suggested.

"What? Those silly gulls?"
Little Dolphin gave his friend a
playful nudge with his tail. "You
know they can't spell."

"I've got another idea," squeaked Milo. "Squids can squirt ink. We could ask Sid Squid and his friends to dye the bay in rainbow colors."

"But squids can only make black ink!" Little Dolphin whistled. "If the water turns black, we won't be able to see anything!"

Little Dolphin began to write a list in the sand with his nose. "Come on," he clicked. "We've got a lot more than the decorations to think about. There's food, games, music...."

"That is a lot to do," whistled Milo, examining the list.

"We could ask our friends to help," Little Dolphin suggested.

"Good idea!" chirped Milo. "We'll go and see —"

"Hi there!" came a voice.

It was Poppy! She was spinning toward them with a determined look on her face.

Little Dolphin wriggled in the sand to get rid of the party list. Milo flapped his tail to help.

"I was wondering where you two were," clicked Poppy. "Anyone would think you'd been hiding from me." She stared at them. "What are you doing?"

"It's ... um ... a new dance," Little Dolphin squeaked as he wriggled.

"It's called the Squiddly Squid," added Milo, swinging his flippers, too. "Want to try?"

"I don't feel like dancing," said Poppy sadly. "It's my birthday tomorrow and no one's remembered. I reminded Oscar just now but he shrugged his tentacles and swam off."

"But we'll all see you tomorrow, Poppy," Milo told her happily. "We're going to —"

"Wish you a happy birthday!" Little Dolphin interrupted, giving his forgetful friend a nudge with his nose.

"I should hope so!" snorted Poppy. "Well, can't stop now. I'm off for a swim around the bay. Coming?"

"Sorry, Poppy," Little Dolphin said. "We can't."

Poppy looked disappointed.

"But, you know what? We'll come surfing this afternoon," he added, before she could ask any more questions.

"All right." Poppy grinned. "See you then." And she swam away.

"Phew!" said Milo. "That was close!"

"And we still have so much to do," Little Dolphin whistled. "Let's ask our friends to help."

Oscar, Fergal the turtle, and Hattie the hermit crab were

delighted to help with the
party.

Hattie waved her claws for
silence. "We could have the party
at the old wrecked ship!" she
clacked.

Everyone agreed that was a
great idea.

"And I'll do the decorations,"
Hattie added.

"I'll help," said Milo.

"I can get the cake," said Oscar the octopus. "And I'll be the waiter."

"No juggling with the plates, though!" Hattie said bossily. Juggling was one of Oscar's party tricks, but when he did it, something always went wrong!

"I'll help with the cake and food, too," said Milo.

"Music," whispered Fergal, nearly disappearing into his shell with embarrassment. Fergal was a very shy turtle, even with his friends. "I know someone to ask," he added, blushing.

"Who is it?" Little Dolphin asked.

But Fergal wouldn't tell. "You'll see," he murmured.

"I'll keep Poppy busy in the morning until everything is ready," Little Dolphin said.

"I'll help," said Milo. Milo wanted to help with everything!

"You'll be too busy helping everyone else, Milo," Little Dolphin told him. "But I will need a signal that the party is ready."

"Right!" squeaked Milo happily. Suddenly, he jumped backward on his tail and wiggled his head as if a jellyfish had stung him.

"Are you all right?" asked Oscar.

"Yes," chirped Milo. "I'm showing Little Dolphin the signal!"

"So that's everything," said Hattie, clicking her pincers happily. Oscar clapped and Fergal gave his tail a shy wiggle.

But Little Dolphin didn't join in. He was thinking hard. Was there something else? Then he remembered. "We've forgotten one very important thing!" he squeaked.

Everyone stopped and looked at him.

"Presents for Poppy!"

# CHAPTER TWO

The five friends looked at one
another. Nobody had thought
about presents!

"What do you think Poppy
would like?" asked Milo.

"Claw mittens," began
Fergal. Then he turned pink and
pulled his head inside his shell.
"Silly me!" came a quivering
voice. "Poppy doesn't have claws."

"Nice idea, though, Fergal," Little Dolphin said.

"I'd get her a glass necklace," clacked Hattie, "if I had enough limpets and barnacles to buy it."

"And I'd buy juggling balls!" said Oscar, tossing some pebbles above his head. They landed on Milo's nose.

"Poppy can't juggle!" clacked Hattie.

"Neither can Oscar!" snorted Milo, rubbing his nose with his flipper.

"What about a shell bag or a coral flute?" Little Dolphin suggested.

Hattie shook her head. "None of us can afford to buy something like that."

The friends slumped miserably on the seabed. What could they do?

Then Fergal's little voice piped up from inside his shell. "We could buy one big present," he said, "if we put all our limpets and barnacles together."

"Great idea, Fergal!" Little Dolphin exclaimed.

Fergal's shell wriggled with embarrassment.

The five friends put their limpets and barnacles in a pile and Hattie counted them. "Eight limpets and fifteen barnacles," she announced happily.

"Milo and I will go shopping later," Little Dolphin said. "We can get something really nice for Poppy with all that!"

After lunch, Little Dolphin went to

get Milo. He carried the limpets
and barnacles in a bag.

Milo rushed to meet him,
swinging something from his
flipper. It was a gleaming yo-yo
made from two polished shells.
"My aunt brought this back for me
from Starfish Cove!" he clicked

excitedly. "It's just like yours, Little Dolphin! But I'm having a little trouble. Mom won't let me practice near her anymore after I broke her best vase and clonked her on the head."

"I'll show you how to yo-yo," Little Dolphin offered. "Then we'll go shopping for Poppy's present."

"Poppy's present?" said Milo. He'd forgotten all about the shopping. "Oh, yes, of course. Plenty of time for that!"

Little Dolphin whizzed the yo-yo smoothly up and down from his flipper.

Milo tried to copy him and

got it caught in a nearby clam.
"I'll try again!" he chirped as Little
Dolphin said sorry to the clam.
The yo-yo flew off into a clump
of sea cucumbers. "Hey, where'd
it go?"

"You're
supposed to
hold on to
the string!"
Little Dolphin grinned.

All of a sudden, something
spun into Little Dolphin and Milo,
knocking them sideways.

It was Poppy — and she looked
annoyed. "I've been waiting ages
for you two!" she whistled angrily.

Oh, no! Little Dolphin and Milo were supposed to be surfing with her — but they couldn't go now. They had to shop for her present!

Then Poppy saw Milo pick something up. "What have you got there?" she asked nosily, forgetting to be annoyed.

"Wow!" she whistled. She was looking longingly at the yo-yo. "I wish I had one! I must be the only dolphin in Urchin Bay without a yo-yo." She sighed. "Come on, let's go surfing."

"Sorry, Poppy," Little Dolphin said, feeling very mean. "I promise I'll go with you tomorrow morning. But we can't go now. We've got ... important things to do."

"Important things to do?" snorted Poppy. "Like playing with yo-yos, I suppose. See you tomorrow, then — if you're not too busy." She stuck her nose up and swam off.

"Poor Poppy!" Little Dolphin clicked. "No one to play with and no yo-yo. But we'll make it up to her tomorrow." Suddenly, he gave a happy chirp.

"At least now we know the perfect present for her — a yo-yo of her own! And I know just the shop to find one."

Hidden Treasure was a dark, mysterious shop, full of wonderful things to buy. Two snooty-looking sea horses were examining the displays. They looked down their

noses at Little Dolphin and Milo as the two friends swam into the shop.

An old catfish padded slowly across the cave floor on his feathery fins. His long black whiskers waved in front of him. It was Mr. Cuthbert, the owner of Hidden Treasure. "Can I help you?" he asked.

"We've come to buy a yo-yo," Little Dolphin squeaked.

"A yo-yo," repeated Mr. Cuthbert slowly. "Very popular item. I had a line from here to the jetty this morning and everyone wanted a yo-yo. It was quite a scene."

"Can we see some, please?" Little Dolphin asked.

"It's going to be a special present," squeaked Milo, "for our friend."

Mr. Cuthbert poked around under the counter and pulled out a small wooden box. He nosed it open. "How about this?" Inside was a shiny yo-yo made of two black oyster shells.

"It's a Triton Tornado!" clicked Milo, jiggling with excitement. "Best yo-yo ever made! Poppy will love it!"

"How much is it?" Little Dolphin asked anxiously.

"Let me see," said Mr. Cuthbert, putting on a pair of glasses and squinting at the box. "Fifteen barnacles and … nine limpets."

"Oh, no," Little Dolphin groaned. "We have fifteen barnacles, but we're one limpet short!"

# CHAPTER THREE

The two friends turned sadly toward the door.

"Wait a minute," called Mr. Cuthbert. "Perhaps I can help."

Little Dolphin and Milo darted eagerly back to the counter.

"Because it's a special present, I'll give you a special discount," said Mr. Cuthbert. "You can have the Triton Tornado for fifteen barnacles and eight limpets."

"Thank you!" Little Dolphin and Milo exclaimed together as Mr. Cuthbert tied a piece of pink ribbon-grass around the box. "Poppy will be delighted!"

The next morning, Little Dolphin woke up extra early. He gulped down a quick breakfast and set off to see Poppy. He'd take her surfing while the others got the party ready. Milo would give him the signal when they were finished. He couldn't wait!

"Hello, Little Dolphin," said

Poppy's mom as he swam up. "Poppy said you were coming — but you're rather early. She's still in bed!"

"I was too excited to sleep, Mrs. Whirlpool!" Little Dolphin squealed. "Poppy doesn't know anything about the party, does she?"

"Not a thing!" said Mrs. Whirlpool. "She thinks everyone's forgotten her birthday! But surfing will cheer her up, I'm sure. I'll go wake her up."

Mrs. Whirlpool came back looking very worried. "Poppy's not there!" she wailed. "I can't find her anywhere!"

"She's probably waiting for me at the shore," Little Dolphin said.

"I don't think so!" sobbed Mrs. Whirlpool. "She's taken her suitcase. She's run away!" Poppy's mom spun around the cave, flippers flapping wildly. "What are we going to do?"

"Don't worry, Mrs. Whirlpool," Little Dolphin said quickly. "She can't have gone far. I'll find her."

"Thank you, Little Dolphin!" said Mrs. Whirlpool, slumping onto a rock. "I'll stay here, just in case she comes back home."

Little Dolphin swam off as fast as he could. Poor Poppy! Where could she be?

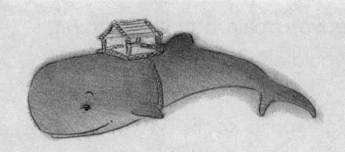

## CHAPTER FOUR

Little Dolphin swam up and down
the reef, looking for Poppy. He
searched the shallows near the
shore. That was one of her
favorite swimming places. But
there was no sign of her.

He looked out at the open
sea beyond Lighthouse Rock.
He felt a shiver of fear run up
his spine. Surely Poppy wouldn't

leave Urchin Bay on her own,
would she?

Little Dolphin swam toward
Lighthouse Rock. As he got
nearer he could see a line
of sea creatures waiting for the
Whale Express. He remembered
when he and his dad had taken
the Whale Express all the
way to Puffin Island to see his
grandma. He'd loved the journey
in the little wooden cabin on

the whale's back. But would
Poppy dare to go on the whale
by herself?

He swam along the line.
There was a family of seals at the
front, and behind them old Mrs.
Periwinkle was gossiping to Mr.
Hawkfish. Then there was a group
of little herrings chattering with
their teacher. The whole line
looked happy to be going on the
Whale Express. All except one.

At the very end was a sad little
figure with a suitcase. It was
Poppy!

Little Dolphin darted
toward her. "Poppy!" he
whistled with relief. "I've
found you!"

"Oh, it's you, Little
Dolphin," said Poppy
gloomily.

"Your mom's really worried,"
Little Dolphin said. "Why did you
run away?"

"Because it's my birthday,"
clicked Poppy, "and no one
remembered."

"Your friends have

remembered!" Little Dolphin whistled, putting a flipper around her. "Come back with me and you'll see."

But before Poppy could answer, somebody barged in between them.

"Morning, Poppy!" said a smooth voice. It was Vinnie, the shiftiest shark in Urchin Bay. He gave Poppy a toothy grin.

Little Dolphin knew that grin. Vinnie had something to sell, and it was sure to be a trick.

"Look what I've got for you!" Vinnie held out a shiny yo-yo to Poppy.

"Oh! Thanks, Vinnie!"
squeaked Poppy. She glared
at Little Dolphin. "At least *someone*
remembered my birthday!"

"It's not a present!" Vinnie
gulped, his eyes popping
with horror at the
thought of
giving
some-
thing away. "But since it's your
birthday, I'll do a swap. You take
this expensive yo-yo and I'll take
your old shell suitcase. Can't say
there's a fairer trade than that."

Poppy looked longingly at the
yo-yo. "Can I try it out?" she

asked.

"No need," said Vinnie hastily. "Trust me, you won't find a yo-yo like it in any shop. Handmade! Great workmanship."

Poppy held out her suitcase, ready to swap.

Little Dolphin didn't know what to do. If only he could tell Poppy about the Triton Tornado. He had to act fast. "Go away, Vinnie!" he said desperately.

"Why?" asked Vinnie, puzzled. "I'm just about to close a great deal here!"

"Er ... your cave's on fire!" *Only Vinnie could fall for*

*something as silly as that,* Little Dolphin thought.

"Blithering barracudas!" exclaimed the horrified shark. "My beautiful cave!" He swam off in a panic, dropping the yo-yo.

The yo-yo sank down onto the seabed — and fell apart.

Little Dolphin took a closer look at it. It wasn't a real yo-yo at all, just two old bottle tops held together with a rusty nail.

Poppy nosed at the pieces that lay in the sand and burst into tears. "This is my worst birthday ever!"

"Never mind, Poppy,"
Little Dolphin said kindly.
"Let's go tell your mom
you're safe and then we'll
go surfing. You will have
fun today. I promise!" Little
Dolphin thought of Poppy's
party with a tingle of
excitement.

Poppy managed a small grin.
"I'd like that!" she said.
The two friends sped
off toward the reef.
As they swam away,
they could hear Vinnie's
voice in the distance.
"Wait a minute!

My cave can't be on fire. It's underwater."

## CHAPTER FIVE

"Whee!" cried Poppy as a
foaming wave took her speeding
along. "This is fun!"

Poppy had gone home, given
her mom a big hug, and promised
never to run away again. Now
she and Little Dolphin were
surfing the Urchin Bay breakers
while Little Dolphin waited for
Milo's secret signal.

The two dolphins chased up and down in the rolling surf, chattering excitedly and catching the best waves to ride.

Suddenly, Poppy stopped and poked her nose above the water. "Look at Milo!" She giggled. "What *is* he doing?"

In the distance, Milo was jumping backward on his tail and wiggling his head as if a jellyfish had stung him. It was the signal. The party was ready!

"Let's see what he's up to," Little Dolphin suggested. He knew Poppy wouldn't be able to resist being nosy.

"Good idea," clicked Poppy. "I was wondering where everyone was. Urchin Bay's not usually this quiet."

They skimmed out toward the middle of the bay. But Milo had vanished.

"He'll be hiding somewhere, ready to jump out on us." Little Dolphin grinned. "Let's surprise him instead!"

"Yippee!" exclaimed

Poppy, spinning with excitement. "I love hide-and-seek."

Little Dolphin led Poppy down toward the seabed, darting behind rocks and bushes as they went. So far, everything was going according to plan. But he didn't want Poppy to see the wreck until the very last minute.

They came to a huge clump of orange cup coral. The wreck was just on the other side. "I bet Milo is hiding behind there," Little Dolphin whispered. "You go first and surprise him."

Poppy dashed around the

coral — and stopped in astonishment!

The old wreck had been completely transformed. The tattered rope rigging was lit by glowing lantern fish. The broken deck was smothered in beautiful sea lettuces and eelgrass. HAPPY BIRTHDAY POPPY

was written in the sand in brightly colored seaweed.

"Who did all this?" squealed Poppy.

There was a loud cheer and all of Poppy's friends and family burst out from their hiding places. Poppy spun herself dizzy with delight.

Suddenly, there was a drum-roll. Everyone looked toward the wreck. On the cabin were three grinning sharks with microphones. Fergal was standing shyly next to them.

"It's the Sharky Sharks!" shrieked Poppy. "I love them!"

The Sharky Sharks launched
into their latest hit.

"Great job, Fergal!" Little
Dolphin exclaimed. "When you
said you'd take care of the music,
I never dreamed you'd be inviting
the most famous band in Urchin
Bay!"

"They live next to my grandma,"

whispered Fergal. "I've known them since I was hatched."

"Let's party!" shouted Oscar, jiggling his tentacles in time to the beat.

The party was fantastic. Everyone danced around the wreck to the wonderful music. Then they played Sardines and Hunt the Kipper until Oscar called them all over.

"I hope you're all hungry," he said, balancing plates of seaweed sandwiches on his tentacles. He juggled the sandwiches above his head and skillfully tossed them to the guests.

"I've been practicing!" he said
with a wink at Hattie.

When everyone had finished,
Hattie clicked her claws for
silence. "Time for the birthday
cake!" she called. She looked
around. "Where is it, Milo?"

"I hid it!" said Milo proudly.

"Where?" Little Dolphin
asked.

"Er ... sorry," squeaked Milo. "I can't remember!"

"You are a scatterbrain!" Hattie chuckled, tapping him with a pincer.

"It's Hunt the Cake time!" called Oscar. "Whoever finds it gets the first slice!"

Everyone jostled and giggled as the search for the cake began.

"I found it!" squeaked Poppy
at last.

She pulled the cake out from
behind the rusty old cannon
that stood on the deck of the
wreck.

Little Dolphin grinned. He
should have known that Poppy,
the nosiest dolphin in Urchin Bay,
would find it!

"Delicious!" said Poppy as
she took a huge bite.

"Birthday cake?" said a
voice. "Then I'm just in time!"
It was Vinnie.

No one had invited the shifty
shark — but that never stopped

Vinnie, especially when he could smell food!

Vinnie barged through the crowd just as Oscar the octopus was showing everyone his latest trick — spinning eight yo-yos at once.

"Help!" yelled Vinnie as eight yo-yo strings wrapped themselves around him. He was completely

trapped. "Get 'em off me! Before the cake runs out!"

"I can't!" said Oscar. "The strings are all knotted."

"Useless things!" snapped Vinnie, wriggling helplessly. "You should have bought your yo-yos from me."

"I did!" Oscar chuckled, and everyone laughed.

There was a clash of cymbals and a beaming Poppy appeared on the deck.

"This has been a wonderful party," she said. "Thank you, everybody!"

"It was Little Dolphin and

Milo's idea," said Hattie.

"But everyone helped," Little Dolphin insisted.

"And it's not over yet!" chirped Milo. He nudged Fergal forward.

Fergal made his way shyly toward Poppy with the wooden gift box on his back. The other friends followed and gathered around as Poppy carefully untied the pink ribbon-grass. She nosed open the box. When she saw the Triton Tornado inside, she simply stared at it with her mouth open.

"Don't you like it?" Little Dolphin asked anxiously.

"We could take it back," added Milo.

"Don't you dare!" exclaimed Poppy. "It's perfect. It's the best yo-yo in Urchin Bay!"

Poppy took the Triton Tornado and spun it around her head. Then, as the Sharky Sharks started their next song, she suddenly began to wriggle in the sand, her tail flapping wildly.

Everyone watched in surprise.

"Are you OK, Poppy?" Little Dolphin asked.

"Too much cake," said Milo.

"Silly boys!" squeaked Poppy, swinging her flippers. "I'm doing the Squiddly Squid! You remember — it's the latest dance. You showed it to me."

"Of course we did!" Little Dolphin laughed. "Come on, everybody! Get wriggling!"

Soon everyone was dancing the Squiddly Squid — even the Sharky Sharks!